10 Minute Tales

The Hero Next Door

When you see these symbols:

Read aloud
Read aloud to
your child.

Read alone
Support your child
as they read alone.

Read along
Read along with
your child.

EGMONT
We bring stories to life

Read aloud   Read along

After finishing his last job at the Pontypandy Fire Station, Sam put away his fire helmet and said goodbye to Penny.

"What will you do today, now that you're off duty?" Penny asked.

"I have some chores to do at home," he smiled. "But first, I'm off to the supermarket. See you tomorrow!"

Whistling cheerfully, Sam headed into town.

Sam finishes his last job at the fire station.
He will do his chores now that he's off duty.

Read aloud   Read along

At the supermarket, Mike the handyman was finishing a job, too. "There, that's better," he said, as he put cement over a crack in the paving behind the shop.

"Thank you," Dilys said, and went to step on the cement.

"Whoa!" said Mike, holding her back. "The cement needs time to set first."

When Mike and Dilys had gone, naughty Norman looked at the wet cement, thinking of a very naughty idea ...

Read alone

Mike fixes a crack behind the supermarket.
The wet cement needs time to set.

Read aloud   Read along

At the front of the supermarket, Mike climbed up his ladder to fix a leak in the roof.

When Sam arrived, Dilys knew he was off duty as he wasn't wearing his helmet. "How are you spending your time off?" she asked.

"I've lots to do. I need to weed my garden, then iron some clothes and paint my front door. But first, I have to buy some things from your shop," Sam explained.

"Come inside!" Dilys smiled.

Sam comes to the supermarket.
Mike climbs a ladder to mend the roof.

Read alone

Meanwhile, Norman found a long stick to draw pictures in the wet cement. Just then, his friend Sarah walked by with her dog, Nipper.

"Want to see something really cool round the back?" Norman asked her.

"Sure!" said Sarah. She tied her dog lead to Mike's ladder. "Wait here, Nipper. I'll be back soon!" she told him.

Norman wants to draw in the cement. Sarah ties Nipper to the ladder and goes to watch.

Read alone

Read aloud Read along

Nipper sat on the pavement. Then he spotted Lion the cat walking past.

"Woof!" barked Nipper.

"Miaow!" Lion yowled, then he ran across the road.

Nipper bounded after Lion, but his lead was still tied to Mike's ladder. The ladder crashed to the ground, leaving Mike hanging from the roof!

"Argh!" shouted Mike. **"HELP!"**

Nipper pulls the ladder down.
Mike is left hanging from the roof!

Inside the shop, Dilys was showing Sam a new iron. They heard Mike's shouts and Sam ran outside. Dilys rushed out too, forgetting to turn off the iron.

"Great Fires of London!" Sam cried. "Hang on, Mike. I'll get the ladder."

He saw Nipper dragging the ladder across the road just as Trevor's bus appeared. Slamming on the brakes, Trevor stopped just in time!

"Well done, Trevor!" called Sam, as he untied Nipper. Just as Mike was about to fall, Sam put up the ladder and saved him!

Dilys shows Sam a new iron. He hears Mike's shouts and fetches a ladder to save him!

Read aloud   Read along

Trevor jumped out of his bus to bring Nipper off the road. "Are you all right?" he asked Mike.

"Yes, thanks to Sam," Mike answered. "I'm lucky he was here."

Sam smiled. But suddenly, Trevor's bus began to roll down the street, with no driver inside!

"Watch out!" Dilys cried.

"Oh no, I must have left the handbrake off!" cried Trevor.

Read alone

Trevor has left the brake off in his bus.
It rolls away without a driver!

Read aloud   Read along

"Stand back!" called Sam as he chased after the bus. The situation was very dangerous – especially if someone was in the path of the runaway bus!

Sam ran as fast as he could to the bus' door. Just as it was about to crash into a house, he jumped into the driver's seat and yanked on the handbrake. The bus jolted to a stop, just a few centimetres from the front door!

"Sam, you saved the day – again!" cheered Trevor.

Read alone

Sam chases after the runaway bus.
He stops it before it crashes into a house!

Read aloud   Read along

As Sam was catching his breath,
he heard more shouts.

"Help, I'm stuck!" cried a voice
from behind the supermarket.

"That sounds like Norman!" said Dilys.

Sam dashed around the back of the supermarket,
with the others following after him.

Norman had been drawing a picture in the wet
cement, but his trainers were stuck now that it
was set! "Help! I can't move my feet!" he wailed.

Norman draws a picture in the wet cement.
But the cement has set and Norman is stuck!

Sam said, "I'll get you out, Norman."
He pulled Norman up until he popped free.

"Norman Price, what am I going to do with you?"
scolded Dilys.

"Sorry, mam," Norman said. "Thank you for saving
me, Fireman Sam," he added.

Dilys went on. "All I ask is a little peace and qui–"

BEEP! BEEP! BEEP!

Suddenly, a loud alarm went off nearby!

Read alone

Sam pulls Norman out of the cement.
Just then, an alarm goes BEEP! BEEP! BEEP!

Read aloud **Read along**

"That sounds like the supermarket's smoke alarm," said Sam.

Dilys gasped. "I must have forgotten to turn the iron off. I'll run in and call 999!"

But Sam stopped her. "Never enter a burning building," he told Dilys. "I'll run back to the station and get help."

The hot iron starts a fire in the shop.
Sam stops Dilys from going inside.

As Sam ran up the street towards the station, he saw James with his skateboard.

"Hi, Sam," smiled James. "I was just – **oh!**"

Before James could finish, Sam grabbed the skateboard and jumped onto it, whizzing up the road. "Sorry, James!" he called. "It's an emergency! I'll bring it right back."

Once at the station, Sam and the crew rushed out in Jupiter, with its sirens wailing.

Nee nah!
Nee nah!

Sam skateboards to the fire station.
The fire crew rush out in Jupiter.

Jupiter screeched to a stop in front of the supermarket and the fire crew jumped out.

"Elvis, shut off the power in the building," Sam ordered. "Penny and I will work the fire hose."

"Yes, sir!" Elvis saluted before he ran off.

Sam and Penny unrolled Jupiter's water hose and turned on the tap. Inside the supermarket, they sprayed the fire with water. They soon put the fire out. Luckily, no one was hurt!

Read alone

Sam and Penny spray the fire with water.
They soon put the fire out!

A short time later, Penny asked, "Did you get all your jobs done on your day off, Sam?"

"No ... but I saved Mike from falling off the roof, stopped a runaway bus, freed Norman from the cement, skateboarded to the fire station, then helped put out a fire!" Sam laughed.

"We're lucky you were here," Dilys told him. "And since you gave up your day off to help all of us, I'll do your ironing and Mike will paint your door. And for being so naughty, Norman will weed your garden for the rest of the summer!"

"Aw, Mam ..." Norman whinged.

"Thanks, everyone," said Sam.

Sam has saved a lot of people on his day off.
So they will help with his chores at home.

Read aloud   Read along

Sam finally headed home after his busy day, but he didn't get far before he heard more cries for help.

"Arrrrgh! I can't stop! **HELP!**" Station Officer Steele came flying down the street on James' skateboard. The skateboard was out of control, but Steele was going too fast to stop!

"Don't worry, sir! I'll save you!" Sam called out as he started to give chase.

As everyone laughed, Elvis joked, "Well, as Sam always says, a good firefighter is never off duty!"

Officer Steele can't stop the skateboard.
Sam goes to save the day one more time!

10 Minute Tales

Enjoy more from the
10-Minute Tales range
Featuring all your favourite characters

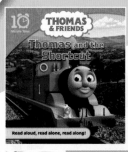

OUT NOW

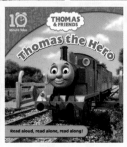

Go online at egmont.co.uk/10minutetales for puzzles, colouring and activities!